All the Animals
Where I Live

To the Littlest Birds

Copyright © 2018 Philip C. Stead

A Neal Porter Book

Published by Roaring Brook Press

Roaring Brook Press is a division of Holtzbrinck Publishing Holdings Limited Partnership

175 Fifth Avenue, New York, NY 10010

The art for this book was made entirely by hand using a combination of techniques including:

oil ink monoprinting, printing from found objects, and drawing with China marker,

bamboo calligraphy brushes, and Sumi ink.

mackids.com

All rights reserved

Library of Congress Control Number: 2017944495

ISBN: 978-1-62672-656-7

Our books may be purchased in bulk for promotional, educational, or business use. Please
contact your local bookseller or the Macmillan Corporate and Premium Sales Department
at (800) 221-7945 ext. 5442 or by e-mail at MacmillanSpecialMarkets@macmillan.com.

First edition, 2018

Book design by Philip C. Stead

Printed in China by RR Donnelley Asia Printing Solutions Ltd., Dongguan City, Guangdong Province

10 9 8 7 6 5 4 3 2 1

All the Animals
Where I Live

PHILIP C. STEAD

A NEAL PORTER BOOK   ROARING BROOK PRESS   NEW YORK

IF YOU FOLLOW THE DIRT ROAD DOWN FROM MY HOUSE, past the family of wild turkeys that roost on the wooden fence, you'll find a ninety-year-old woman who lives all by herself.

One day the old woman saw a bear from her kitchen window.
So she went outside—

"SHOO!"—

and scared away the bear.

I used to live in a busy city.
From my kitchen window I could see
buses and trains,
people waiting for buses and trains,
ambulances rushing to the hospital,
dogs on leashes walking to the park,
people arguing, and people holding hands.
I never saw a single bear.

Now I live in the country.

But still I haven't seen a bear.

Not unless you count Frederick. This is Frederick.

My Grandma Jane gave me Frederick when I was three years old.

Now he sits nearby while I write stories and draw pictures.

Sometimes, when I don't know what to draw, I just draw Frederick.

I loved my Grandma Jane.

There was a room in her house that always smelled like maple syrup.

I don't know why.

On the bed was a wool blanket made from lots of squares all looped together.

In each square was a chicken.

Grandma Jane knitted that blanket herself.

When I would stay overnight I would sleep underneath the chickens.

If my Grandma Jane had been an animal
she would have been a hummingbird—

flitting and buzzing and always busy,
gathering fluff and knitting it into a comfortable nest.

She would introduce herself to all the animals in the neighborhood.

Then she would fly to where I live now.

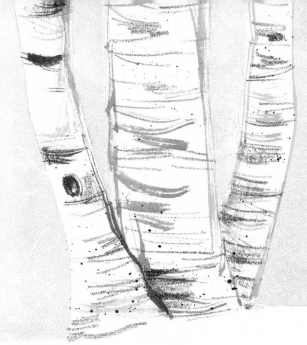

There are a lot of animals where I live.

But the most important one is my dog. Her name is Wednesday.

Wednesday is not from here. She is from the pound in Baltimore.

Wednesday has lived in a lot of places, but this place is her favorite.

Here, in the summertime, she can sit by the bird feeder
and look across the field to where the apple trees stand.

In the morning the cranes come and make a racket.
A toad opens one eye to have a look.
But it is already too hot and too loud for a toad.
He goes back to sleep while the dragonflies buzz.

An eagle drops a turtle from high up above.
The turtle lands on its back in the tall grass.
The eagle is upset. But the turtle is happy.
He begins his long walk home.

At night it is quiet.
But only until you listen.
There are a lot of little things playing their music in the moonlight.

Then the coyote howls, and nothing moves.
Except for Wednesday.
She runs to the window and barks, barks, barks.
Wednesday echoes through the dark field,
over the apple trees,
and into the woods where the coyote disappears for a while.

Summer comes and summer goes.
The wind knocks the apples to the ground.
Wednesday knows that the deer will come.
She waits and chases them away. It is a game they play.

The chipmunks make their home in a hollow stump.

In winter Wednesday watches out the window.

The cranes have all flown away.

The mice and moles are hiding underground.

The littlest birds huddle together and share seeds that fall from the feeder.

When the wind blows they fly away in a hurry.

Then there is nothing but snow.

And the smell of maple syrup.